The Story of Santa Claus

THE · STORY · OF ·
Santa Claus

by Tom Paxton
illustrated by Michael Dooling

MORROW JUNIOR BOOKS · NEW YORK

Oil on canvas was used for the full-color illustrations.
The text type is 14-point Goudy.

Text copyright © 1995 by Tom Paxton
Illustrations copyright © 1995 by Michael Dooling

Printed in Singapore at Tien Wah Press.

1   2   3   4   5   6   7   8   9   10

Library of Congress Cataloging-in-Publication Data
Paxton, Tom.
The story of Santa Claus/by Tom Paxton; illustrated by Michael Dooling.
p. cm.
Summary: Claus enlists a family of elves to help make toys for children in the Old Forest, but when the cottage
becomes too crowded, they move to the North Pole, beginning the tradition of delivering toys
to children around the world on Christmas Eve.
ISBN 0-688-11364-8 (trade) — ISBN 0-688-11365-6 (library)
1. Santa Claus—Juvenile fiction.   [1. Santa Claus—Fiction.   2. Christmas—Fiction.]   I. Dooling, Michael, ill.   II. Title.
PZ7.P29212St 1995   [E]—dc20   94-23919   CIP AC

For Midge
—T.P.

For Bill Leeds
—M.D.

On a night made darker by the boughs of the tall pine trees, a burly figure plowed through deep drifts of snow. The stars were clear in the sky; the moon was beginning to rise. Its first light revealed a much smaller figure at the man's side, an elf of the Old Forest named Arn, darting over the surface of the snow with scarcely any effort at all.

The man smiled at something his companion said, shifting a gleaming woodsmen's ax from one shoulder to the other. Some snow was shaken loose from a fir tree as he passed, and he shivered as it drifted down his collar. Onward he plowed, leaving a wide track in the snow.

He paused on a hilltop to wipe his brow, which was tanned from years out-of-doors. His eyes were bright, and his white hair stuck out from under a red wool cap. His beard flowed down to his chest.

His name was Claus, and he had spent his whole life in the Old Forest, first in the home of his parents and now in his own cottage with his dear wife, Eva. He was a forester, just like his father had been, and looked after all things, both plant and animal, that lived and grew in these woods. It was his ax that cleared away the old and dead trees and made room for the new saplings, and it was he who returned young birds fallen from their nests to safety. Fawns who had strayed were shown the way home, and squirrels were directed to the juiciest nuts on the ground.

Again he stopped and lit his pipe, calmly puffing on it. Then he continued his journey till he reached the clearing in which his small cottage stood. Arn left him there with a wave and a parting word. Claus strode up to the cottage, brushing the snow from his boots and coat. Eva heard him and came to open the door. She was as tiny as Claus was large. Quick in her motions, she cleaned the last snow from his back. Laughing softly, she said, "Off telling tales to the children again?"

"It's true, Eva." Claus smiled. He hung up his heavy coat and sat down at the table. "Wherever I go, they seem to find me and ask for a story. All I do is tell them stories the elves have told me."

When Claus had finished eating dinner, he thanked Eva and turned his attention to his toys. Something happened when Claus picked up his knife and a good piece of wood. His blade would flash, and soon little soldiers stood at attention, fairies held slender wands, and puppies seemed ready to wag their tails. Claus had learned the art of carving toys from his father; ever since, he had spent the long autumn nights before the fire, whittling. It passed the time pleasantly, and it delighted the children of the Old Forest to receive the toys.

Claus's knife blade began to send shavings snowing to the floor. He worked quickly—and a good thing, too, for such was the popularity of the old man's toys that children from miles around knew them and wanted them. Each child in the Old Forest knew that every year he or she would receive a new toy made by the old forester. Each year more children learned of these marvelous toys and spread the word, until Claus had to work longer and longer hours to fill the need. Later and later into the nights he worked; faster and faster he whittled. Now he was growing weary.

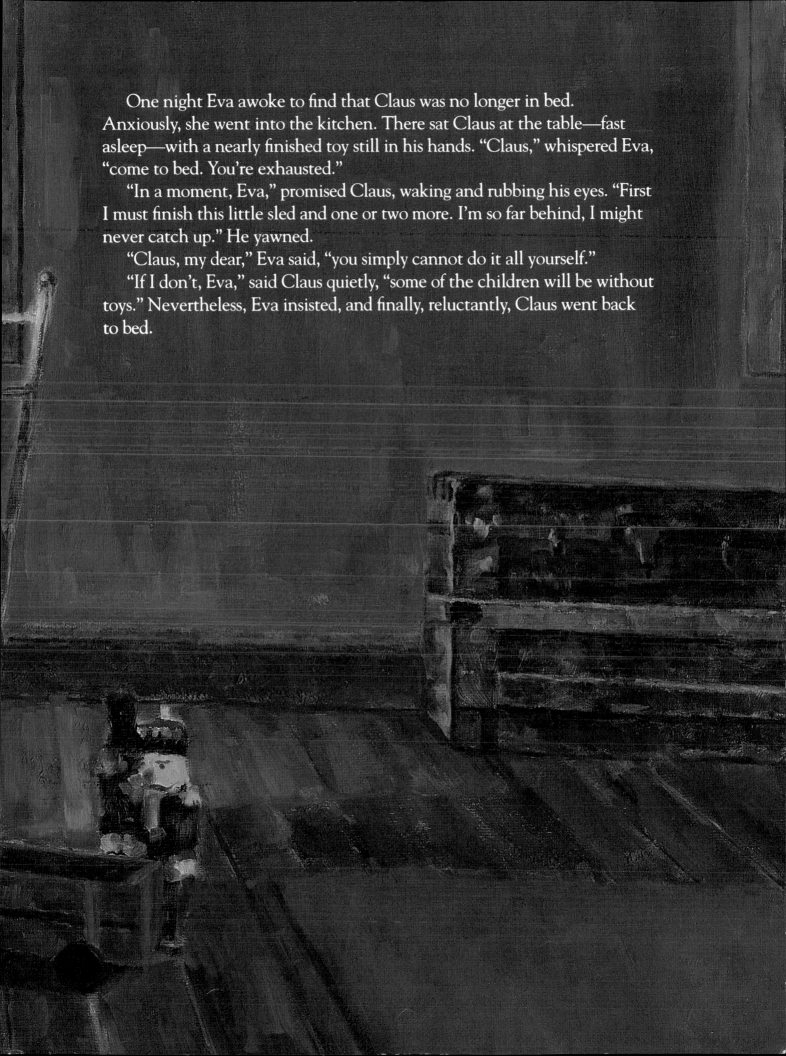

One night Eva awoke to find that Claus was no longer in bed. Anxiously, she went into the kitchen. There sat Claus at the table—fast asleep—with a nearly finished toy still in his hands. "Claus," whispered Eva, "come to bed. You're exhausted."

"In a moment, Eva," promised Claus, waking and rubbing his eyes. "First I must finish this little sled and one or two more. I'm so far behind, I might never catch up." He yawned.

"Claus, my dear," Eva said, "you simply cannot do it all yourself."

"If I don't, Eva," said Claus quietly, "some of the children will be without toys." Nevertheless, Eva insisted, and finally, reluctantly, Claus went back to bed.

In the morning, to his great surprise, he found the completed toy sled on the table. Did I finish it after all? he wondered. I was so sleepy that I can't remember. His puzzlement only increased when he saw that the runners on the little sled were pointed in the wrong direction. Claus shook his head in bewilderment.

The next night, however, it happened again: A toy soldier, half-completed when Claus went to bed, was done when he came in for his breakfast. Claus held the little soldier in his hands and turned it around and around. "Eva," asked Claus, "have you been finishing my work for me while I sleep?" Eva shook her head.

That night, when she saw that Claus was asleep, Eva slipped into her boots and her heavy cape and quietly left the cottage. Hours later she returned, smiling to herself.

The next morning, Claus was sitting at the table when someone knocked on the door. Rising slowly, he crossed to the door and pulled it open. Standing in the clearing was a crowd of elves, none taller than Claus's belt buckle. The elves regarded him silently for a moment. All at once they broke into a high-pitched babble, the sound of which made Claus laugh. They flowed around the startled old man into the cottage. There was Arn, who had walked with Claus in the forest. There was Hans, who was quite stout, and there was Oola, whose straw-colored hair hung down her back in an enormous braid. Soon the sounds of sawing, hammering, and nailing filled the room. Eva came in her dressing gown to gaze in quiet happiness at the hive of activity.

"You knew of this, Eva?" asked Claus.

Eva nodded. "I've been friends with Oola for years," she confided. "We met when we were both berrying one summer day. I knew that if I really needed her, she'd come—and all her family with her. Now, what do you think?" she asked.

"I think I know *now* who was finishing my toys while I slept," said Claus.

Quickly the elves began to produce toys. They had set to work with great earnestness, their faces knitted in concentration. It was apparent, however, that most of the elves had more enthusiasm than skill. The toys looked all right, but they seldom worked properly. Some of the wagons had only three wheels, toy soldiers had little shovels instead of muskets, and the dolls had their dresses on backward. Claus had to call for silence, gather his new assistants around him, and show them patiently what to do. The elves proved to be very fast learners, and soon they were turning out perfect toys at a terrific rate.

That year there were toys enough for every child in the Old Forest. But Claus and the elves were making them in such great numbers that a new problem arose. The cottage had become so crowded that there was no longer room for Claus and Eva. There were toys in the parlor, toys in the kitchen, and toys on the bed. One day Claus attempted to cross the parlor and could find no place to put his foot. He tried to step to one side—no room. Trying to step back, he tripped over a stack of dollhouses and crashed to the floor. Luckily he wasn't hurt, but clearly this would do no longer. Claus looked at Eva as he sat among the splintered houses and said, "My love, the cottage is simply bursting with toys, and we haven't room to turn around. I must think of something!"

Claus spent the day in thought, twice going for long walks in the forest. Finally he returned, smiling, with the look of a man who has reached a decision. "Eva, the time has come to say good-bye to the Old Forest," he said. "I've decided we must move to a new home with room for all of us—toys, elves, everyone."

In the morning the sounds of packing filled the clearing, and soon wagons full of furniture, toys, pots and pans, clothing, and tools stood before the cottage. By midday they were finished loading, and Claus, Eva, and the elves took a last look at their old home. As they made ready to leave, several children watched with fretful faces. "Don't worry, children!" called Claus. "I won't forget you!" With that, they drove the wagons up the road to the north.

For days they trekked, until the snow grew so deep that the wagons could go no farther. That night no one could sleep, so loud was the sound of Claus's hammering and nailing. In the morning they saw that Claus had replaced the wheels with skis. They piled into the wagons and swept over the snow into the forest again. Northward the group went for many days more. At last Claus raised his arm to halt the wagons. "We are here," he said. "This is our new home."

They looked about them. All was snow and ice, with a brilliant blue sky above, but it seemed as if at just this spot the snow was even whiter and the

sun shone even brighter. Indeed, there was something quite special about
this very spot. "Why, Claus," said Eva, "this is beautiful! Where are we?"

"It's the North Pole," replied Claus.

They set to work at once. The snow flew as they unloaded the wagons.
Hans and the other elves cut great blocks of ice that Arn used to build walls.
In a short time their new home stood gleaming at the North Pole. There
was room now for everything and everybody—room for toys, for elves, and
for Claus and Eva, too.

Months passed, and one evening Eva said to Claus, "I love it here, but now and then how I miss the trees of the Old Forest!" How astonished she was the next evening when a great commotion erupted at the door. It flew open, and in burst Claus, Arn, and Hans, dragging a great green fir tree. Quickly they stood it in the corner in a pot of water. "Just like the Old Forest, Eva!" said Claus, setting down his ax and smiling at her delight. "I found a grove of these trees not far from here, and I've been planning this surprise for months."

"Oh, thank you, Claus!" said Eva. "Thanks to all of you." Then she grew thoughtful. "Now wait, everyone! I have an idea." Dashing to her room, she returned with her sewing basket. She began to place bright snips of colored ribbons in the branches. Everyone got the idea, and soon buttons, little silver balls, and tiny toys also hung from the tree. Strips of silver paper looked very much like icicles. And ropes of popcorn swung from branch to branch. Oola fashioned a star that Claus placed on the treetop. They stood in silence then, admiring the festive tree.

The elves worked hard, and Claus invented many new toys. Still, he wondered how he could deliver them all. "We're so far from the children," Claus said. "How can I reach them from here? And what of the other children?" he added. "We have room now to make toys for all of them. They should all have toys."

Day after day Claus gave the matter a great deal of thought. At last he smiled. Then out the door Claus went, through the blowing snow, until he disappeared. When the sun set, he still had not returned.

For two days Eva and the elves waited impatiently for a sign of him. It was Christmas Eve, and without Claus no one knew what to do about the children and their toys.

At last they heard jingling bells and a shout of "Hello-o-o!" They ran out into the snow, and there sat Claus in a gleaming red sleigh with eight handsome reindeer in a harness hung with bells. Claus laughed at their surprise. "Look at the beautiful reindeer that live here. Once I explained to them what I needed, they were eager to help." The reindeer pawed the snow. "It was building the sleigh that took time." Claus laughed again. "But now I'm ready to go! Bring me the toys!"

Quickly the elves brought a gigantic bag and put it behind his seat. It was large enough to hold the entire year's supply of toys. "There's no time to waste," shouted Claus. "We have little time and far to go." He called to the reindeer, "In the old days I walked, but tonight we're going to have to fly!" He snapped the reins and whistled. One, two, three steps the reindeer took, and then off they flew into the starry sky.

Throughout that night Claus landed his sleigh on rooftops all around the world. Down each chimney he plunged, bag of toys in hand, only to emerge moments later with a bit of soot in his beard. Off he flew again, from house to house, town to town, country to country.

Next morning the boys and girls awoke to find Claus's toys, and somehow each toy seemed perfectly chosen for each child who received it.

It happened again the following Christmas and every Christmas thereafter. Yet neither Claus nor Eva nor any of the elves grew older as the years passed. The more they worked at their toy making, the younger they seemed to get and the happier they were. As for the children, Claus had become their Santa Claus, and to this day they look to Christmas morning, knowing their dear friend will not forget them. He never has, and he never will.